2/08/2021

To Maeve & Rally,

Happy reading!

Lots of love,
    Uncle Francis & Aunty Geraldine
            X X

ULSTER LEGENDS

NICOLA HEANEY

PETER HEANEY

ILLUSTRATED BY CONOR BUSUTTIL

THE O'BRIEN PRESS
DUBLIN

About the Authors

NICOLA HEANEY was born and raised in Derry. After studying in Scotland, she taught English Literature in Bristol and Madrid for over a decade before deciding to focus on her writing. Her poetry has been published in various journals across the UK and Ireland, but this is her first collection of stories.

PETER HEANEY was a primary school teacher in his native Derry for forty years. During this time, he also worked with the Department of Education, developing literacy and storytelling projects; this work attracted several Irish, UK and European awards. As part of the inaugural UK City of Culture in Derry, he initiated a major storytelling and cultural exchange programme with Derry City Council and the Oracle Corp. using video conferencing and virtual learning between schools in Derry and Kentucky, USA. Peter has also worked with The O'Brien Press for several years, creating teaching resources and guides to support the use of class novels across the curriculum in developing a range of skills and learning experiences.

About the Illustrator

CONOR BUSUTTIL is a children's picture book illustrator and passionate doodler. Originally from a small rural village in County Down, he currently lives in the Welsh valleys. He was recently selected by the Eric Carle Museum as a rising star. Conor also illustrated *The Children of Lir: Ireland's Favourite Legends* by Laura Ruth Maher, published by The O'Brien Press.

Dedication

For Nuala, Matthew and Andy,
with thanks for the support, encouragement and good humour they gave us.

CONTENTS

THE RED HAND

Once, before the time of Saint Patrick, Ulster had no king for more than a year.

The chieftains met in the Brehon assembly (*ancient Irish court*) but they could not agree on a leader. The arguments became more bitter and angry.

Diarmuid, a fierce and fearless warrior, had the support of the Eastern clans. Heremon, cunning and determined, had support from the Northern clans. The druids were afraid that one of the chieftains would snatch the leadership without agreement. This would cause years of misery and violence. They suggested approaching the High King, Conaire Mór, at Tara. Conaire's decision would be accepted.

Each chieftain chose someone to go to Tara. Erímhón was clever with words. He could tell what people thought by listening carefully to what they said. He held the trust of Heremon. Diarmuid sent Cathal Mór whose mood could change within a heartbeat.

Conaire Mór entertained them with a week of feasting and games. They had competitions in running, jumping, wrestling and target practice. Each evening, they all ate and drank together while listening to the king's bards and musicians.

Conaire Mór and his druids watched their guests very carefully and learned a lot about their characters. They agreed that the Ulstermen were proud and very capable men. They would only follow someone who could do something extraordinary that they themselves could not.

'Strength alone will not be enough,' said Conaire. 'One of them must find a way to show that his courage and determination are greater.'

The druids suggested a great contest in which these qualities would reveal themselves clearly.

That evening at the banquet, Conaire announced:

'The lordship of Ulster will be decided by a great sea race from Rathlin Sound across the Sea of Moyle to the sandy beach at the foot of Glenshesk.

'The first chieftain to lay his hand on the beach will be raised as Lord of Ulster. No champions may be used, and those who would be lord must crew the course with their men, each boat to hold no more than five crew.'

And so at the Celtic festival of Bealtaine (*1 May*), the crews gathered on Rathlin Sound, waiting for the druid's signal.

There were nine boats and crews, each hoping to claim lordship. They all knew this coast well. They knew that the short journey across the Sea of Moyle held many dangers. There were fierce rip tides and jagged rocks, hungry to rip apart any boats that strayed off course.

As the druid lowered his staff to signal the start, the crews strained on their oars. The boats leapt across the sound and out into the dangerous waters. Immediately the eastward-sweeping tides seized them, dragging them towards the towering sea cliffs at Fair Head.

The crews pulled on the heavy oars, dipping and straining through the crystal green waters flecked with dancing sea horses.

The day was calm but the tidal rip was unforgiving and scattered the crews. Finally, only Diarmuid's and Heremon's boats were left, jostling each other as they raced into the final stage. The black basalt slopes of Crockaneel reared up before them at the head of the glen, marking the end of the race.

Despite the efforts of Heremon's crew, Diarmuid's boat was in the lead as they rowed through the shallow approach to the beach. Sure that the prize was slipping from his grasp, Heremon remembered Conaire's exact words, as reported by Erímhón:

'Lordship will fall to him whose hand first touches the beach.'

Laying his hand on a rowing block, he took his war axe and, with one swift swing, cut his own hand from the arm at the wrist. Ignoring the pain, he grabbed the severed hand from the deck and hurled it with all his might towards the beach, ahead of Diarmuid's boat.

Heremon's hand fell on the beach at the feet of the druid, just as Diarmuid's boat crunched on the shingle. Diarmuid jumped out to claim the lordship.

But the druid lifted the bloodied hand and held it up before Diarmuid, declaring:

'This is the hand of Heremon, first to touch the beach. I proclaim him rightful Lord and King of Ulster.'

Diarmuid, his face a kaleidoscope of his feelings, bowed slowly. The other crews and chieftains then filed past the druid, who was still holding Heremon's bloodied hand, to salute their king.

Ulster accepted Heremon as its leader. His action is still remembered today: a red hand is the symbol of Ulster and is also on the Tyrone GAA crest.

THE GREAT BROWN BULL

It was a beautiful sunny morning. Donn Cúailnge stood at the top of the hill, looking down over the green fields of County Armagh. Life was good.

It had not always been like this. He had once been a man — a pig-herder who spent his days arguing with his enemy, Rucht. Then one day a magician had changed them into two great bulls, one brown and the other white.

Donn Cúailnge, the great brown bull of Cooley, now belonged to Daire MacFiachna, Ulster's richest cattle-herder.

Sometimes, Daire brought visitors to see Donn. They usually brought gifts. Donn liked their gifts.

Daire had not come for a few days. Donn asked Sorcha, one of the cows, if she knew where he was.

'Don't you know, Donn?' Sorcha was delighted to know something Donn didn't.

'If I knew, would I be asking?' Donn snapped. As a human, he had been grumpy. As a bull, Donn got very angry very quickly.

'He's organising the defence of our lands,' Sorcha snorted. 'Queen Maedhbh of Connacht plans to steal you away.'

Donn pawed at the ground. 'As if I would go to Connacht! The grass here is the best in the land.'

A raven sat on the stump of an old oak tree. She looked at them both with a sharp eye.

'The battle has begun,' she said. 'Can't you smell the blood? They will take you, Donn Cúailnge, or they will die trying.'

'Let them die!' roared Donn.

The raven laughed. She was no ordinary bird, but Morrigan, the goddess of war. Her hobby was causing death and anger. She made Donn so angry that he could not control himself.

Donn tore through the valley, ripping trees from their roots. After a while, he saw Maedhbh's camp. With a loud bellow, he charged through the fences. Swinging his huge head left and right, he ripped through the camp. He was at the door of Maedhbh's tent before the Connacht warriors managed to control him. By then, he had trampled fifty soldiers into the ground.

Tied to a huge oak tree, the great brown bull strained and bellowed. When anyone came near, he charged them. The rope that held him cracked. Suddenly he heard a voice he recognised.

The bravest of the Ulster warriors had arrived: Cú Chulainn. He was the only warrior who could defend Ulster against Maedhbh's army.

'I've come to reclaim that bull!' Cú Chulainn shouted. 'Hand him over and leave with your lives.'

'You are one man against an army,' they said. 'Go back to Ulster before we kill you!'

Cú Chulainn's sword killed fifty Connacht men that day.

Meanwhile, charging with all his strength, Donn snapped his leash. He charged through the Connacht ranks, escaping into the forest.

For two days, the bull went wherever he wanted. He bathed in cool streams when he felt too warm. He slept in the shade of huge leafy oak trees when he felt tired. He munched on sweet grass when he felt hungry. It was heaven!

On the morning of his third day of freedom, Donn heard voices. It was a man and a woman — and they were arguing. Unafraid, Donn stepped out of the trees and into the path.

The woman jumped down from her horse and ran towards him, arms open.

Donn let the woman rub his nose. He was glad of the attention. He snorted in pleasure as she tickled the hair between his eyes.

'You are a magnificent big beast, aren't you?' she said. 'The best in all of Ireland! We have had so much trouble looking for you and here you are. Well, Donn Cúailnge, you will be coming home with me to Connacht. You will live there like a king — just as you deserve!'

Donn was excited to hear that he was going to be treated like royalty. He was also looking forward to getting nice food.

The cart was comfortable and the woman gave Donn lots of treats. On the third day, a huge castle appeared over a hill. This was to be his new home.

As they got closer to the castle, Donn noticed a strange smell. It grew stronger and stronger. When he saw a huge meadow, he suddenly remembered. That villain Rucht! He had heard rumours he was in Connacht. He was now the white bull Finnbennach.

Donn bellowed and jumped from the cart. Across the meadow, a white shape moved closer. It was Finnbennach. Donn let out an ear-splitting roar. He charged towards his enemy.

Because of his long journey, Donn Cúailnge was not very fit. Finnbennach was well able for him. The two bulls lowered their heads and charged again. And again. And again.

They fought all day and all night. They charged around Ireland, their horns locked in their fight to the death. At dawn, Donn Cúailnge limped out of the trees. The remains of Finnbennach hung from his horns.

Then, with a snort, Donn turned his back on Connacht. He was going home.

Halfway across Ireland, Donn left the body of his enemy in a field. Then he headed north to Ulster. As the mountains of Mourne grew larger, he walked faster. He was expecting a great welcome. After all, hadn't a whole war been fought over him?

When his hooves hit Daire's land, Donn sped towards the main house.
As he ran, panting heavily, his huge chest grew tighter and tighter. Suddenly
his heart gave out and he collapsed, killed by the effort. His body was
carried back to Daire.

People came to County Armagh from far and wide to see the famous
Brown Bull of Cooley. They sang songs about his legend.

THE HORSEMEN OF AILEACH

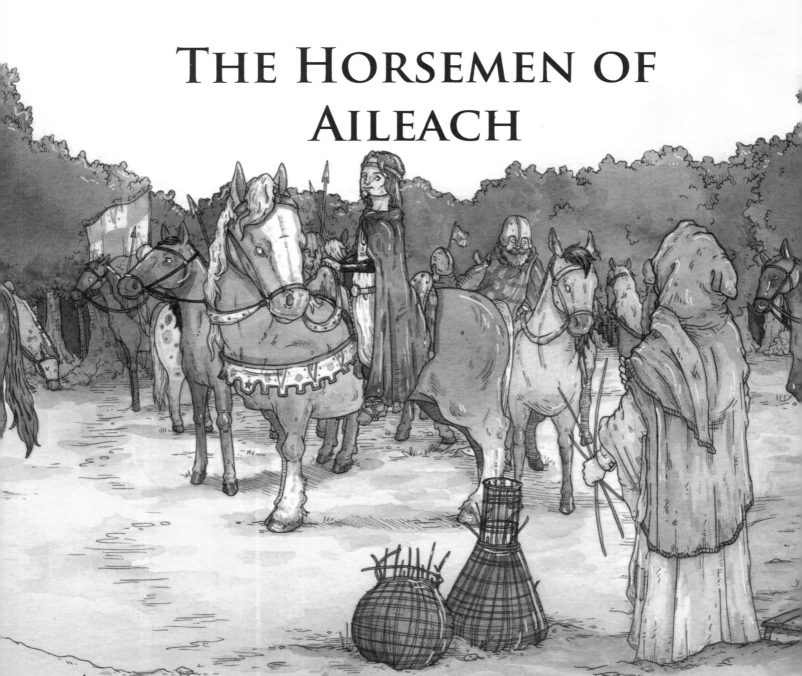

Áine was mending a fishtrap when she heard the hoofbeats. She laid the fishtrap aside and waited.

Suddenly, a small group of well-dressed horsemen burst from the trees. Áine gasped — their leader was wearing a crown!

Áine stepped out to greet them. She knelt as she got closer.

'Good morning.' The voice was gentle. 'I have come this way to speak to the great sea god, Manannán Mac Lir. We seem to have lost our way. Can you help us?'

'Of course, your majesty,' Áine said. She pointed towards the trees behind their house. 'If you follow the path through these trees, you will get to the shore.'

Áine felt the king's gaze upon her. 'Maybe we should take you with us to show us the way,' he said. Áine wished her brothers could see this!

One of the king's men lifted her onto the back of his horse. Then he swung back onto the saddle in front of her.

She put her cheek against the man's back and closed her eyes. The trees whizzed past. Soon she was giggling with excitement. When they broke from the forest, the sea spread out in front of them. Áine whooped in joy.

'It's wonderful, isn't it?' the man said, smiling. 'I remember the first time I rode a galloping horse. I felt like I was flying.'

The High King stood on the shoreline. His arms were raised. He was calling to Manannán Mac Lir.

Suddenly, the waves began to swell. They had almost reached the height of the trees when a white horse appeared, galloping through the surf towards the beach. Soon, it was followed by another … and another … until the beach was filled with white horses. On every horse sat a warrior, straight-backed and proud. It was the white horsemen of the Tuatha Dé Danann. Manannán Mac Lir had woken them to answer the High King's call.

The warriors began to move in circles. They moved faster and faster until Áine was dizzy watching them.

With the High King leading them, they galloped away from the sea, their armour shining in the evening sunlight. They were heading south to drive the invaders from the shores of Erin.

'We will leave you home,' Áine's companion said. 'But you must promise never to tell anyone what you have seen.'

Weeks passed and Áine kept her promise. Sometimes she thought she had imagined the whole thing!

One night she dreamt about a magic mountain. When she woke early, she thought she heard the faint thunder of hooves. Checking that the rest of the family were asleep, she tiptoed out of the house. Could the horsemen be returning? Outside, the noise was louder. Hooves — and lots of them!

Áine ran to the stable. She had been secretly practising riding their only horse. Now she managed to get the stubborn mare to move. They trotted quickly towards the sea.

The noise of hooves grew louder and louder. Áine got down and tied the horse to a heavy branch. She was trembling with excitement.

Sure enough, it was the white horsemen. Their leader rode out over the waves. His men were lined up along the shore. But something was wrong — the waves were pushing him back to the beach!

The horse staggered out of the waves. The soaked warrior was clinging to his back. Áine looked more closely at the band of riders. There were dents in their armour. They looked more human than before. They had paid a price for their victory.

As the men waited on the shore, a voice echoed across the dunes:

'Congratulations! You have driven the invaders from our shores. Your home is no longer beneath the waves. It is under the hill of the sun god. Go now and do not bother me again!'

And so, the Tuatha Dé Danann left the sea. They rode silently through the dunes to the sacred hill at Grianán of Aileach in County Donegal. The top of the hill shimmered in the light of the rising sun.

Slowly, each of the horsemen faded from view. The Hill of the Sun God wrapped itself around them. It led them into its deep tunnels. They lie there to this day, resting until Ireland needs them again.

PAISTE

When Ronan opened his eyes, the sky was dark. He was in his favourite place — a clearing deep in the Mullaghclogher forest. This was his thirteenth summer and he liked to lie on the cool grass and daydream.

Usually, he could tell the time by where the sun was. Today the clouds were too thick. Suddenly he realised: not clouds, but smoke!

He leaped up. Sure enough, there was a smell of burning. He scrambled up a tree for a better look. Angry red flames rolled over the woodlands on the other side of the valley. There was a trail of scorched earth behind them. Paiste was back!

Ronan scrambled down and hurried back towards his village, running so fast his chest hurt. He burst out of the trees and skidded to a halt. There was just a charred rectangle where their house had been. He fell to his knees, crying.

It was getting late and Ronan knew that with Paiste around, it was not safe to be outdoors. He got up and began the long walk to Aunt Siobhán's village over the mountain. Her husband was the chieftain there.

When he arrived, the moon was out. Aunt Siobhán gave him a bowl of delicious hot stew and explained that his family had escaped.

When he had eaten, Ronan settled into a bed in the great hall and watched the shadows cast by the fire dance on the walls.

After a while, the village elders came in. Ronan snuggled deeper into his furs and listened. They were talking about Paiste.

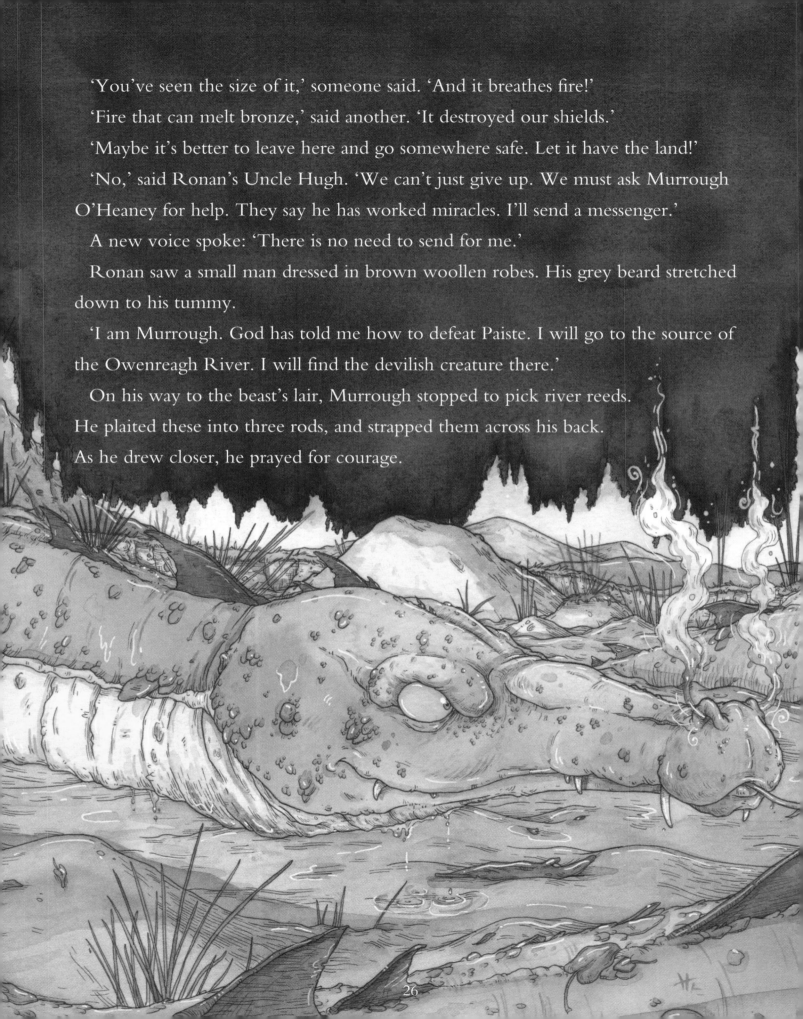

'You've seen the size of it,' someone said. 'And it breathes fire!'

'Fire that can melt bronze,' said another. 'It destroyed our shields.'

'Maybe it's better to leave here and go somewhere safe. Let it have the land!'

'No,' said Ronan's Uncle Hugh. 'We can't just give up. We must ask Murrough O'Heaney for help. They say he has worked miracles. I'll send a messenger.'

A new voice spoke: 'There is no need to send for me.'

Ronan saw a small man dressed in brown woollen robes. His grey beard stretched down to his tummy.

'I am Murrough. God has told me how to defeat Paiste. I will go to the source of the Owenreagh River. I will find the devilish creature there.'

On his way to the beast's lair, Murrough stopped to pick river reeds. He plaited these into three rods, and strapped them across his back. As he drew closer, he prayed for courage.

The shallow pool was partly hidden by leaves and tall reeds. There was no sign of life no birdsong, no rustling undergrowth, no ripples in the green water. A deathly silence hung over the valley.

Suddenly, the water began to ripple. Two terrible yellow eyes focused on Murrough and narrowed threateningly. Coil after coil of the serpent's scaly body unfurled from the water. Paiste's lips drew back, showing two sets of glittering razor-sharp teeth.

'What have we here?' said Paiste. 'A tasssty morsssel for me to eat?' Paiste's forked tongue flicked in and out of his mouth.

'The villagers sent me to pay homage to your greatness,' Murrough said. 'To complete my ritual, I will lay these rods in a wreath around you.'

A curl of smoke escaped from Paiste's nostril as he hissed, 'Rodsss? Ritual? You do undersssstand that I will eat you anyway, little mortal?' The scales on his hide glittered emerald and turquoise in the afternoon sun.

Murrough moved closer. He placed one rod on the serpent's left. Then he rushed around to the other side. When the third rod touched the scales on Paiste's back, Murrough made the sign of the Cross. Then he closed his eyes and prayed.

The air bubbled with energy. Paiste shrieked.

When Murrough opened his eyes, the terrible beast was trapped in a steel cage. God had changed the reeds to steel. Paiste pushed against the bars, but he could not free himself.

'Sssssssset me free!' cried the worm.

Murrough's voice boomed through the valley:

'You have sinned for long enough, murdering people and destroying their homes. It is God's will that you remain bound for eternity.

'Pleassse!' said the serpent. 'Let me see the Ciannacht from my prissson.'

'I will bring you to Lough Foyle,' Murrough said. 'You will remain there for eternity, unable to murder or destroy. From there you will be able to see the Ciannacht.'

It was late afternoon when Murrough got back to the village. Ronan heard people celebrating and went to the river.

'You are safe now,' Murrough told the villagers. 'God's will has been done.' The crowd cheered.

Ronan noticed a rope held tightly in Murrough's hand. The other end was in the river. As he watched, the water began to ripple.

While everyone was celebrating, Murrough slipped away. The rope trailed behind him. Ronan ran along the riverbank to catch up with him. Murrough heard the footsteps and turned round. His grey eyes bored into Ronan.

Ronan blushed. 'I'm sorry,' he said. 'It's just — I saw that you had something on the rope. I wanted to see what it was.'

The corners of Murrough's mouth twitched. 'I was trying to keep it a secret,' he said. 'Paiste is at the end of this rope — imprisoned in a cage. I'm taking him to where the Foyle opens up to the sea.'

Ronan gaped at him. 'All that way? Alone? How will you manage to find shelter or food if your hands are tied to that rope? Let me come with you and help.'

Murrough smiled at the boy. 'I've been praying to God for assistance,' he said. 'Now I see that he has sent you.'

Side by side, Murrough and Ronan walked off along the riverbank. Paiste was dragged along beside them in the water. It took time but they finally reached Lough Foyle and cast him into the depths.

They say he struggles against his cage still, causing unusual currents and high tides in the lough. If you look very closely, maybe you can see him under the surface.

THE GREAT BLACK PIG

Long ago, before the time of the great Cú Chulainn, there was a school on the Cavan–Leitrim border. The teacher was called Master Donn. He was a small, crooked, cruel man.

The Cavan boys were the youngest in the class. They were bullied by the bigger Leitrim boys. Master Donn encouraged the bullies. He was a bully too.

Each Friday, the children came home tired, with their clothes dirty and torn.

When asked what they had been doing, they would say: 'Ach, sure it was only running and jumping.'

Their parents saw no harm in running and jumping.

That is, until that final Friday in June, the day when the Great Black Pig appeared.

That morning, the class was quiet. The boys were looking forward to the end of term. There would be no more running or jumping for eight weeks. If Fergal's plan worked, there would be no more running or jumping ever again.

Fergal had lost the seat of his trousers to the fangs of Donn's hounds. Now he would teach Master Donn a lesson he would never forget.

Sitting very still and silent, the boys waited. They heard the master's heavy steps approaching. His cruel eyes flicked across the class and fell on Conal, a gentle boy who was small for his age.

'Ah, Master Conal,' he said. 'I believe it is your turn to provide the sport for us today. Am I correct?'

Before Conal could answer, the master pulled a twisted twig from his jacket. Then he muttered a dark spell and waved the twig at Conal.

As Donn's evil spell fizzed around him, Conal's thigh muscles swelled with power. His thigh bone grew longer. It pulled the bottom of his trouser legs up almost to his knees. Then he dropped on all fours and ran to the door. He was now a large hare.

As Conal skidded through the door, the master hissed a second spell. Hearing the barking and baying of hounds, Conal bounded across the playground.

He jumped the school wall into the fields. It took all his skill to stay ahead of the snapping jaws and vicious fangs of the pack. He ducked through hedges, jumped across ditches and dived under bushes. His trousers were in tatters when he arrived back in the classroom. But he had survived in one piece.

The Leitrim pack tumbled though the door after him, still snarling and snapping. Donn waved his twig to change them all back to their own shape.

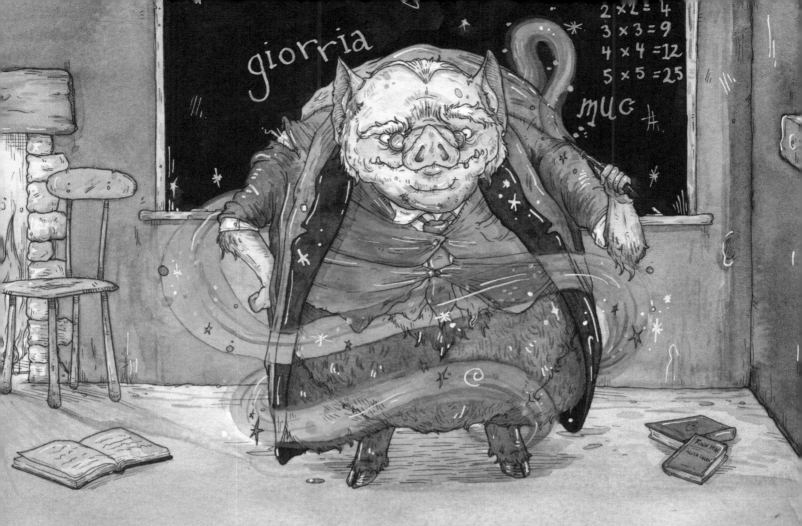

When the master's wild laughing had calmed, Fergal asked: 'Master, is it only children you can change?'

'I can shape-change whoever I want,' Master Donn snarled.

'Could you change yourself?'

'Of course,' snorted Donn. 'Will I change into a mighty lion? Or an eagle?'

'I've heard that one of the hardest creatures to change into is a pig,' Fergal said. 'A black pig.'

Donn eyed him darkly. Then he pulled the twig from his jacket and waved it over his own head, muttering.

At once, he dropped to the floor. His hands and feet were trotters. His back and belly shook like a jelly as he grunted. Black hairs sprouted around his evil snout.

When Donn dropped his twig, Fergal seized it. He snapped it in two in front of his eyes. Then he threw it onto the fire.

The stove bulged as it swallowed the twig with a great roar. A huge belch of coloured sparks thundered from the chimney. The fire ate the twig and scattered its magic across the roof and into the air.

Donn's eyes filled with horror. He knew that they had fooled him. He was trapped inside the black pig. Howling with rage, he charged around the room. He knocked all the desks and chairs over.

As he bolted through the door, the Cavan boys' cheers rang in Donn's ears. His Leitrim gang stumbled after him. They tried to help, but only got in his way and made him even more angry.

For weeks, he charged through the countryside from dusk to dawn. He rooted up huge trenches and ramparts with his great bristled snout. When at last he reached the coast, he was never heard from again.

To this day, you can see the trenches and ramparts he dug up across Cavan and Leitrim. If you listen closely, you might just hear the echoes of Master Donn's evil squeals.

MAEVE MACQUILLAN

Maeve MacQuillan was her father's only child, and the light of his life. The halls of Dunluce Castle in County Antrim rang with the sound of her laughter, as she skipped through the rooms. One day, she pulled back a heavy tapestry and found a locked door.

A deep voice called from the other side of the door. 'Hello?'

Maeve jumped back, startled. 'Hello? Who's there? I'm Maeve.'

'Hello, Maeve. I'm Reginald.'

Maeve sat down against the door and began to chat. Reginald was kind and funny. Maeve sat for hours every day, sharing her dreams with her new friend.

Weeks passed. One day, Maeve heard footsteps on the stairs. Her friend Aoife pulled aside the tapestry and found her.

'What are you doing, Maeve? You're not allowed in this part of the castle! Certainly not with that *O'Cahan* in there.'

Maeve knew that there was a blood feud between her father and the O'Cahan clan but she didn't care.

She ignored Aoife's advice and continued to visit Reginald. They talked about how they would spend their life together once he was released.

Then one day she sneaked up the stairs to find the door open and Reginald gone. Filled with fear, she ran through the castle to find her father.

As she approached the great hall, she ran straight into him. 'Maeve, sweetheart!' he said. 'Look who's here!' Lord MacQuillan grinned as he took his daughter's arm and brought her into the huge room.

Despite her emotions, Maeve knew how to greet guests, and she curtseyed politely. Rory was a distant relative who had been visiting them for a year. Whenever she tried to speak to him, he turned the colour of a squirrel and mumbled into his boots.

'You remember Rory Óg?' Lord MacQuillan said. 'Any man would be happy to welcome him as a husband to his daughter.'

Maeve's heart fell. Horrified, she ran from the hall to her bedroom.

'It's so unfair!' she sobbed into her pillow.

Minutes later, her father threw open the door

'That's no way to behave,' he said. 'Rory is young, wealthy and kind! He will make you an excellent husband. In two moons' time, you will be his wife.'

Maeve's temper was as fiery as her hair. She lifted her face from her pillow and cried, 'I will not marry him! I love another — Reginald O'Cahan! I would rather die than marry anyone else.'

Lord MacQuillan's face turned purple. 'That man I just released? No daughter of mine will marry one of the O'Cahan family. You'll marry Rory Óg or you can live in the tower!'

'Fine!' Maeve shouted. 'I'll go there right now!'

She marched the familiar route, head held high.

The days passed. Aoife brought food three times a day and tried to persuade her to work on her bridal robes but Maeve was too angry to listen. After a few weeks, her father came to visit.

'You silly girl!' he thundered. 'Have you come to your senses yet?'

Maeve turned to him, her face thin and pale. He looked at the white fabric on her lap.

'It's my funeral shroud,' she said. 'I'm sorry, Father. I can't marry Rory. I'll die if I can't marry Reginald.'

'You must marry Rory,' Lord MacQuillan said. 'I can't break a bond with a kinsman. I can't be seen to allow you to marry another. But…'

Maeve held her breath.

He looked thoughtful.

'… if you ran away to marry Reginald, then I would not have broken my word.'

After a week, Maeve's father knocked on her door. 'It's been arranged,' he whispered. 'Reginald thinks that I will be away this evening. Be ready.'

Maeve kissed her father on the cheek. 'Thank you, Father. I will miss you!'

Her father smiled, a little sadly. 'The next time we meet, you will be a married woman! Now remember, be ready by nightfall.'

As the birds outside started roosting, Maeve changed into her bridal robe and sat patiently at the window. Before long, she heard strange sounds from outside. Soon there he was, swinging his legs over the window ledge.

'Reginald!' Maeve rushed into his arms.

Clinging to his back, she squeezed her eyes shut as they climbed down the tower. She could hear the sound of the waves on the rocks far below.

At the bottom, Reginald took her hand.

'Come, my love,' he said. 'Let's start our lives together. I have a boat around the corner. We need to move quickly in case we're caught.'

42

Maeve wanted to tell him everything but nobody must know that her father had broken his bond with Rory Óg. As they climbed into the little boat, a cloud moved in front of the moon. Maeve shivered in her thin bridal robe.

The boat jerked out into the open sea as Reginald rowed away from her home. If Maeve had looked back, she would have seen a figure at her father's window, a hand raised. Instead, she faced forwards, thinking of her future with the man she loved.

Suddenly, a strong gust whipped up the sea around the boat, covering them in spray and pushing the boat back towards the rocks. Reginald lost hold of one of the oars. As he reached for it, another wave hit the bottom of the boat, throwing them both overboard into the icy water. Reginald's body was found on the shore.

Maeve was never seen again. Some say her wedding dress dragged her to the bottom of the sea. Her ghost still wanders the tower, crying out for her lost love. If you listen carefully, you can hear her wail on nights when the moon is full.

FINTÁN ESCAPES

Noah could not sit still. He kept looking to the sky for a sign.

He had been building the ark for many years and still it was not ready. The local people thought that he was mad and laughed at him.

Each day, Noah would pace up and down outside, nodding his head and waving his arms. His wife knew that he and God were chatting about the ark.

One morning, Noah spotted the sign he was looking for. He saw a cloud in the sky. It was neither very big, nor very dark. No one else noticed it, but Noah knew that it was time to get ready.

Noah gathered his sons and told them that it was time to leave. He explained that after the flood, there would be no one else left in the world. They would have to start all over again when the water level fell.

However, there wasn't enough room in the ark. Some of them would have to sail to other parts of the world.

Noah turned to his son Bith and said, 'You must sail west. You will find an island on the edge of the great ocean. It is almost like Eden, but a little colder and wetter.'

Bith hugged his father and set off.

When he reached Ireland, Bith saw that all his father had said was true.

With Bith was his daughter Cessair, two men and forty-nine women.

Cessair was very bossy. Soon her father and the two other men, Ladra and Fintán, were looking after all the women, from early morning till late at night.

They always had chores for the men to do. There was always cooking or washing or fixing that needed to be done. There was no rest for the three men.

As time went on, Bith, Ladra and Fintán got more tired.

The first to die was Ladra.

They were all very sad, but nothing changed for Bith and Fintán. In fact, things were worse, because now they had to do Ladra's chores as well as their own.

Then Bith became so tired that he simply fell over and died too. Fintán buried him on the top of Slieve Breagh.

Each day, the women walked past his grave and placed a small stone on top of it. Little by little, the pile of stones grew bigger and bigger. Even in death, the women seemed to want Bith to carry an unfair load.

Fintán did not want to die like Bith and Ladra and then have to carry a load of stones on his head for the rest of time, so he made up his mind to escape.

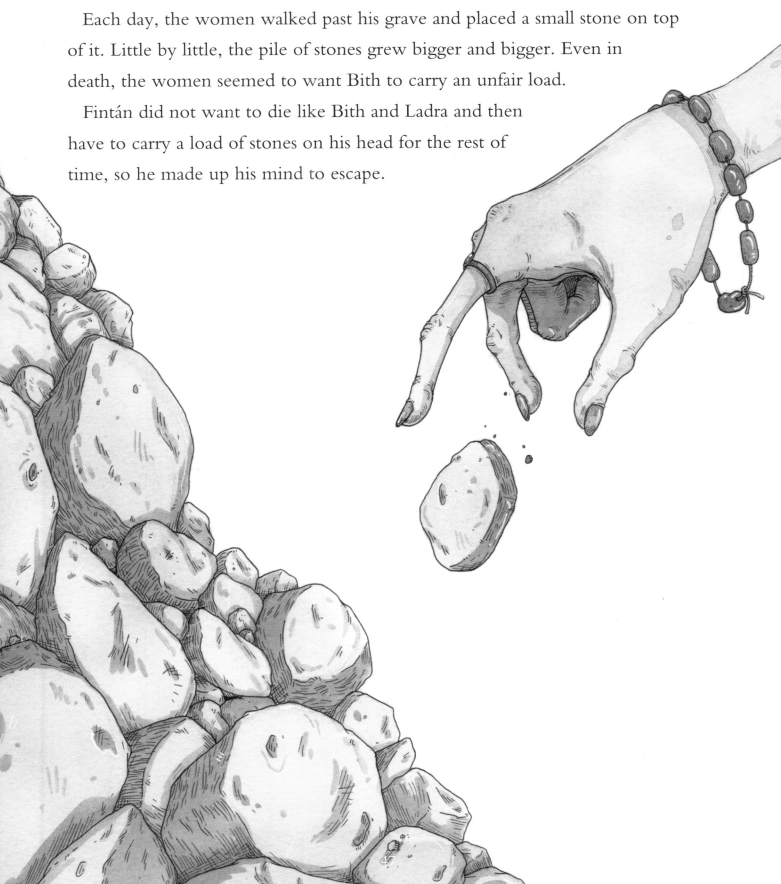

Fintán knew that the women would never allow him to escape. He was the only man left.

They kept him so busy that he had little time to think. But he knew that the women hated water. They had wanted to live in County Monaghan because it was so far from the sea. Fintán knew that they would never allow him to reach the sea.

Then he thought of the well. It was always his job to fetch the water. He did all the cooking and washing. The women never got their hands wet.

Next morning, he made up his mind to escape. When he reached the well, the women with him stayed back in case they got splashed.

Fintán took a deep breath and leaned into the well with his bucket. He leaned further and further then tumbled into the water at the bottom.

When he hit the water, he changed into a graceful silver salmon that arced through the water like a shining arrow.

When the women plucked up their courage to peep into the well, Fintán was nowhere to be seen. All they could see were the scales of the salmon flashing silver in the gloom.

With a final flick of his tail, Fintán swam into the depths of the well and freedom.

Many hundreds of years later, Fintán, the salmon, met the hero Fionn Mac Cumhaill, but that is another story.

FEBOR AND FIA

One Spring afternoon, Febor was walking through a forest in County Fermanagh. The sun was shining. The forest floor was covered in bluebells. Everywhere, there was life and colour. But Febor saw none of this as she stamped along the paths.

She had been to visit Baron O'Phelan. His castle in Boho was one of the biggest in the county. She had told him to stop being greedy. She said that if he followed Christ, he could change his life — and the lives of his people. But he laughed at her and her holy books. He said he would set his dogs on her if she came back!

Febor turned to check on her pet deer, Fia. Fia followed Febor everywhere. Her big eyes were gentle and full of love. Across her back was Febor's satchel, filled with her holy books.

Soon, they left the forest and began to cross a large meadow. Febor started to notice the beauty. Two butterflies danced past her. Their red wings shone in the afternoon sun. She stopped to admire the wild cornflowers. As she did so, she noticed something else. It was the sound of barking. Febor and Fia paused, listening as the barking grew louder and louder.

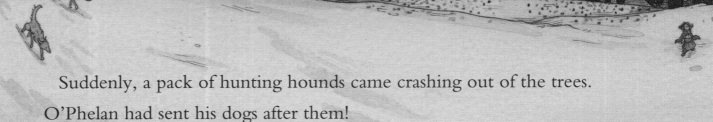

Suddenly, a pack of hunting hounds came crashing out of the trees. O'Phelan had sent his dogs after them!

The hounds were close enough for Febor to see saliva dripping from their sharp teeth. Then Fia started to run. The dogs were snapping at her heels and leaping at the satchel across her back.

Febor knew that O'Phelan didn't like her spreading the Lord's message. But would he try to destroy the holy books? She rushed after them.

'Go, Fia! Don't let them catch you!' Febor shouted. She had never seen dogs hunt before. But she had heard that they never gave up.

From the top of the meadow, Febor could see for miles around. Fia was in the valley. She was surrounded by snarling dogs. The river Sillees was behind her. It was fast and dangerous.

'Fia!' Febor screamed her friend's name. She ran down the hill, almost tripping on the way. Halfway down, Febor stopped to catch her breath. She watched in horror as Fia turned to make her way across the stepping stones to the other bank. Febor's heart was in her mouth. She watched helpless as Fia stumbled. The deer was washed downstream by the current.

Febor ran towards the river as fast as she could.

When Febor reached the riverbank, Fia was standing there, soaked. Water dripped from the satchel on her back.

Horrified, Febor dashed over to her beloved pet. She unbuckled the satchel. The holy books were ruined!

'I'm sorry, Fia said. 'I had to cross the river to lose the dogs. The current dragged me in. I tried to protect the books, but the water was too strong. It felt like there was something trying to drag me under — and I don't mean the current!'

Febor stroked her pet's neck. 'I'm not angry with you,' she said. 'But the river should have known better. I've heard tales about a demon in the river…'

Fia looked at Febor. Her big brown eyes were wide with surprise. 'A demon? I thought I was imagining it, but … I saw a pair of red eyes when I was pulled into the river.'

As she flicked through the soaked pages of her books, Febor was furious. 'This should not have happened,' she said. 'These books are sacred.' Trembling with rage, she flung up her arms and turned towards the river.

'You have ruined the sacred books of Febor!' she shouted. 'I curse you for it. From this day your flow will change. You will never again empty into the sweet waters of the wild Atlantic. Forever you will be imprisoned in the dark water of Lough Erne. No fish will find a home in your foul waters. Hear me and let this be done!'

The water level began to rise. Huge waves crashed against the banks. Whirlpools appeared, growing deeper and deeper. Suddenly, a face appeared, red and twisted in anger.

'I knew it!' Febor cried. 'This river was home to a demon. That's why my books were ruined. Well, no more!'

With a shriek, the face disappeared as the demon was pulled down into the whirlpool and destroyed.

Then slowly, the river became calm. The water level returned to normal.

Behind her, O'Phelan's hounds were whining. Febor turned to find herself face to face with the Baron himself.

'You set your hounds on me.' Her voice was calm. 'You broke your promise that I would be safe as long as I never returned.'

'No harm has been done,' the Baron said. 'Now get off my land and take your deer with you.'

O'Phelan turned his horse and began to move back towards his castle, his dogs following behind him.

'No harm was done?' Febor could not believe what she had just heard. 'My sacred books are ruined!'

O'Phelan did not turn to answer.

'You have destroyed my most precious belongings,' cried Febor. 'So I will destroy yours! I curse you, your land and your castle!'

With this, the sky began to darken. The ground around O'Phelan's castle began to shake. Within minutes, the castle had disappeared completely into the earth.

Today, if you visit Boho, you will find no trace of Baron O'Phelan's castle — and no sign of life in the Sillees River.

COLMCILLE AND THE BOOK OF MOVILLA

When he reached the top of the Munro (*high mountain*), Colmcille was exhausted. He gazed out over the horizon, praying that this time they had sailed far enough and that he would no longer be able to see any sign of Ireland.

He had vowed to be an exile, so he could no longer watch the sun change the colour of his beloved Donegal hills or sink into the Atlantic Ocean beyond its mighty western sea cliffs. He would never hear the birdsong of his native land again. It had been a hard decision to accept.

When he closed his eyes, he remembered the battle screams from Cúl Dreimhne. His pride had been to blame for the deaths of so many on that terrible day.

Finnian's book of psalms was beautiful. It was in the monastery at Movilla in County Down. Colmcille remembered when Finnian showed it to him, opened on the altar at the first psalm. The light on the colours brought the words to life. The animals decorating the letters chased each other across the pages. He was spellbound.

Finnian was delighted that his friend admired the book. He was proud that his monastery held such a treasure.

Colmcille wanted his own copy of the book more than anything else in the world. Without Finnian's permission, he crept into the tiny chapel every evening and took the book back to his cell. There he worked long into the night, copying it.

On the last night of his stay at Movilla, someone saw strange lights and shadows flickering in Colmcille's cell. Finnian rushed to investigate. One glance at the manuscript, the inks and the scattered pages told him what Colmcille had been doing secretly. Finnian felt betrayed. As he stormed out, he told Colmcille to leave the original book of psalms and the copy in the scriptorium in the morning.

Before dawn, Colmcille replaced the book of psalms on the altar, bowed and left the church. When he brushed past Finnian, their eyes locked in silent anger. He did not leave the copy he had made. He would never give it up.

Images of King Diarmuid's court and the trial flooded back to Colmcille now.

The court was a dark, pagan place, packed and stinking. There were people there who hated Colmcille and wanted him to be brought low. Colmcille was a chieftain of Donegal. He felt that Diarmuid had no right to judge him.

When Diarmuid rose from his seat, the court fell silent.

'I have reached my decision,' Diarmuid said. '*To every cow its calf. To every book its copy.*'

Glaring directly at Colmcille, he continued, 'You WILL return the copy to Finnian today.'

Colmcille was furious. He would not simply give the copy to Finnian. He would settle this as an O'Neill chieftain … on the battlefield.

'The copy is mine,' he shouted. 'I crafted it. If you will have it, you must take it from me on the battlefield.'

It had been easy to persuade other chieftains to join him and raise a great army. And that day at Cúl Dreimhne, they defeated Diarmuid. No one could take the copy from Colmcille now.

However, as the sun dipped into the sea, and as the darkness cloaked the dead from sight, Colmcille knew he had been wrong. His pride had brought misery to many.

As he stretched again to look out over the sea, Colmcille remembered the vow he had made that night: 'To leave Ireland forever and never to set eyes on her shores again'.

Confident now that the shores of Ireland could not be seen even from this highest point on the island, he returned to his monks. They were huddled around a fire they had built on the beach. They were trying to keep warm as the wind tugged at their damp, salt-stained cloaks.

Aware that they were looking anxiously at him, he sighed and faced them. Then he announced that the shores of Ireland could not be seen from the top of the Munro. At last, they could build their monastery and begin their new lives here on Iona.

First published 2020 by The O'Brien Press Ltd
12 Terenure Road East, Rathgar, Dublin 6, D06 HD27, Ireland.
Tel: +353 1 4923333; Fax: +353 1 4922777
E-mail: books@obrien.ie
Website: www.obrien.ie
The O'Brien Press is a member of Publishing Ireland.

ISBN: 978-1-78849-217-1

Acknowledgements
Thanks to our editor Emer Ryan at The O'Brien Press who guided us through the process with great patience and
direction. Also thanks to Theresa Loftus at the Monaghan County Library and Francis McCarron, storyteller, for
their help with the Monaghan story.

7 6 5 4 3 2 1
24 23 22 21 20

Printed and bound in Poland by Białostockie Zakłady Graficzne S.A.
The paper in this book is produced using pulp from managed forests.

Published in

DUBLIN

UNESCO
City of Literature